D0340244

★PRINCESS★ PROTECTION PROGRAM

The Junior Novel

Adapted by Wendy Loggia
Based on the Teleplay by Annie DeYoung
Based on the Story by David Morgasen and Annie DeYoung

New York

visit us at www.abdopublishing.com

Reinforced library bound edition published in 2011 by Spotlight, a division of
ABDO Group, 8000 West 78th Street, Edina, Minnesota 55439. This edition
reprinted by arrangement with Disney Press, an imprint of Disney Book Group,
LLC. www.disneybooks.com

Printed in the United States of America, Melrose Park, Illinois.
042010
092010
 This book contains at least 10% recycled materials.

Library of Congress Cataloging-in-Publication Data
This title was previously cataloged with the following information:

Loggia, Wendy.
Princess protection program the junior novel / Adapted by Wendy Loggia.
  p. cm. (Princess Protection Program)
 I. Title. II. Series: Princess Protection Program.

[Fic]--dc22   2009926901

ISBN 978-1-59961-746-6 (reinforced library edition)

All Spotlight books have reinforced library binding and are
manufactured in the United States of America.

Chapter 1

*A*nother morning, another bait hook, Carter Mason thought as she sat behind the cash register. Most girls spent those precious minutes before school began doing their hair, texting their friends . . . but not Carter. She didn't even get the chance to hit the snooze button. Joe's Bait Shack was always busiest in the morning. It was a full-service tackle shop. They offered custom rods, bait, tackle, and even rental boats. Being that "Joe" was her dad *and* that she needed spending money, well . . . here she was, working the early-bird shift.

She was thumbing through a catalog, eyeing a gorgeous silk chiffon dress when suddenly, a plastic bag of night crawlers plopped onto the countertop.

"Aw, man!" Carter exclaimed, as some muddy water sloshed out on the counter. She frowned as she looked up at her customer.

"Donny," she said, quickly recovering her cool. Carter had had a major crush on him since the third grade. "Hey."

He looked at her, a confused expression on his face. "Hey . . . uh . . ."

"Carter," she provided. It was a little frustrating that Donny couldn't remember her name when he saw her every day.

He grinned. "Right. How much?"

Carter shrugged. "Oh, no charge," she told him. "A deal's a deal." That had been the best business decision she'd ever made: giving Donny free bait in exchange for a ride to school.

Donny grabbed the bag. "Great."

Carter watched him walk away. Then she took a deep breath, stuffed the catalog into her backpack, and hurried out the door behind him.

"Bye, Dad," she called to her father.

Mr. Mason was busy racking canoes in the small boat-rental area next to the Bait Shack. "Carter, can I see you a minute?" he called.

Biting the inside of her lip, she jogged over. Didn't her dad realize that Donny was in a hurry?

"So," her dad began. "Did he ask you to that homecoming-dance thing yet?"

"Dad!" Carter mumbled under her breath, mortified. She'd been counting down the days to the big homecoming dance—she didn't need her father to do it, too. "Please don't embarrass me."

He gave her a big smile. "I'm your dad. It's my job."

With a sigh, Carter turned and headed toward Donny's convertible. As she approached the car, she realized there were already two other people there. She gritted her teeth. Her biggest annoyance, Chelsea Barnes, sat in the passenger seat, looking as pretty and perfect as she always did. Chelsea's best friend, Brooke, sat in the back.

Carter watched as Donny tossed the bait into a cooler in his trunk, then jumped into the driver's seat.

"Um . . . what are they doing here?" she asked, arching an eyebrow.

"Donny's driving us until I get my new ride," Chelsea announced. "Isn't that sweet?"

"Sweet," Carter repeated flatly, glancing at the backseat. It was covered with dresses. "Um, there's no room for me, Donny."

He looked over his shoulder. "Sure there is. Climb in."

"No, she's right," Chelsea said. "Brooke's already wrinkling my after-lunch outfit."

Brooke scooted closer to the door and frantically tried to smooth out the dress. "I am not!" she squealed.

"It's high school, Chelsea, not Vegas," Carter pointed out. "You don't need a costume change."

"Right," Chelsea said slowly. "But *you* might want to think about it."

Before Carter could think of a comeback, Donny turned on the engine. "Sorry, Carter," he said with a shrug. "But hey, thanks for the bait." And then the convertible peeled out of the gravel parking lot.

Beeeeep! Startled, Carter turned. Her dad was in his truck, ready to drive her to school.

This morning was definitely not going the way she had planned.

"*I* can't stand them," Carter said as she stared out the window at the passing Louisiana countryside. "They're such princesses."

Her dad glanced over at her as he drove. He sighed. "Carter, they're just teenage girls. They're probably just jealous."

"I'm pretty sure they're not," she said, imagining Chelsea and Brooke in Donny's car, giggling, laughing, and hanging on his every word.

Eeeep. Eeeep. An alert sounded. Carter's heart sank. It wasn't a sound she liked to hear. It meant her dad would be leaving for another assignment.

Her father slipped a headset over his ear and punched a button on the dashboard. It flipped up to reveal a hidden compartment with a LCD screen that flickered to life.

"It's Mason," her dad said to the person on the other end, his voice serious. "Yes, sir. No, sir." His eyes met Carter's. It was obvious to both of them what was coming.

"Right away," he said. He pressed a red button, and the LCD screen closed up.

"You're leaving again?" Carter asked.

"Two days, max," he assured her. "It's no big deal. Just a routine op."

Carter snorted. "That's what you always say."

"But this time it's really true," her father said quietly.

Carter wanted to grab his arm and never let him go. She wanted to scream in frustration. She hated when he left her. But instead she said, "Be careful, okay?"

"Always."

The truck pulled up to the front entrance of Lake Monroe High School. Mr. Mason looked over at his daughter. He hated to leave her, too, but he knew she was a tough kid. He lifted his hand, and Carter did the same as they did their traditional good-bye fist bump.

"You and me, pal," Mr. Mason said.

"You and me, Dad," Carter replied. Then she threw her arms around her father and gave him a tight hug. Saying good-bye got harder every time.

And what made it even harder was that her father wasn't going fishing. Or even on a regular business trip.

Her father wasn't just Joe the Bait Guy. He happened to have a side job. Joe Mason was a top secret agent for the International Princess Protection Program.

Chapter 2

$\mathcal{M}$iles away from the Masons' home in Louisiana, the Costa Luna Royal Palace courtyard was elaborately decorated from top to bottom. After all, it wasn't often that a royal coronation was held. Flags flew proudly, ceramic urns overflowed with gorgeous blooms, the red carpet had been rolled out . . . not a single detail had been spared.

Inside the palace, a beautiful young woman stood with her chin held high, a beaming smile on her face. A royal guardsman stepped forward to announce her to her subjects.

"Her Royal Highness, Rosalinda Marie Montoya Fiore. *Princesa de Costa Luna*," he called out.

Rosalinda held back a giggle. The ornate gold-leafed throne room that the guardsman, Dimitri, was addressing was almost empty. This was not her actual coronation; it was only the dress rehearsal.

"And you're walking, walking, as your adoring subjects welcome you . . ." Dimitri instructed.

There was a burst of eager applause from the palace staff as Rosalinda walked gracefully into the room, the skirt of her sunflower-yellow silk chiffon dress swirling. Even the chef and his assistants halted their preparations at the buffet table to clap as she approached the throne on its crimson-carpeted dais.

"Dimitri, my coronation is one month away," Rosalinda said, stopping. "Why do we have to practice now?"

"Because everything must be perfect," he replied.

Just then, one of Rosalinda's favorite people entered the room. It was Señor Elegante, her dress designer.

"*Princesa*, what a beautiful coronation dress you are wearing," he said, his eyes dancing. "Who, may I ask, designed it?"

Rosalinda smiled. "You did, Señor Elegante."

"So I did," Señor Elegante agreed. "I am brilliant, no?"

Rosalinda laughed. "Look. Chef is bringing out the food for tasting. Help me pick the dessert."

"I live to serve, *Princesa*," he said, extending his arm. They walked over to the buffet table, where the chef had set out a huge platter of fresh fruit—pineapple, melon, strawberries—and a variety of cakes for dipping into the massive chocolate fountain that continuously flowed with dark, creamy chocolate.

Rosalinda selected a bright red berry and dipped it into the chocolate. If all the desserts were as yummy as this one, she thought, taking a delicate bite, it was going to be an impossible choice.

"So that's General Kane?" Mr. Mason asked from a balcony high above the throne room. He stood in the shadows with Rosalinda's mother, Sophia, and stared down at a commanding-looking man dressed in a formal military uniform. He himself was dressed as one of the Palace's royal guardsmen—all part of his cover here in Costa Luna, where his latest assignment had brought him.

"Dictator of Costa Estrella, sister country to Costa Luna," Sophia replied. "He has always felt that our two countries should become one—under his rule, of course."

Mr. Mason nodded. "Got a healthy file on him. He's a little early for the party."

They watched as General Kane glanced over at Rosalinda, who was tasting a soufflé with Señor Elegante. She looked up then and gave her mother a wave.

Sophia waved back, her smile bright. "Now that my husband has passed away, only she can

11

become queen of Costa Luna."

"Why Rosalinda?" Mr. Mason asked, curious. "Why not you?"

"I was a peasant girl who married the king," Sophia explained. "Rosalinda is of royal blood. She alone can be queen." She drew in a deep breath. "It is so much for someone so young."

There was no doubt in Mr. Mason's mind that Sophia was under a great deal of stress. But he was there to ease her worries and fears.

"I'll take care of her, Sophia," Mr. Mason assured her.

Sophia's eyes filled with gratitude. "I know you will, Major," she said, placing her hand on his arm.

The orchestra struck up the royal processional, and Mr. Mason nodded at her. "That sounds like your music."

With a nod of her own, Sophia walked regally down the steps to join Rosalinda on the red carpet below. "General," she said as she passed by General Kane.

"Sophia," he said.

"*Vamos*, Mama!" Rosalinda called out happily, glad to have her mother by her side. The two women walked to the dais where the archbishop stood next to the throne. In his hands was a glittering, jewel-encrusted crown.

The archbishop motioned for the orchestra to stop playing. "And now, turn to face your subjects, Rosalinda."

She turned to the room. The palace staff had been hastily assembled to stand in for a crowd of royal subjects.

"Honored guests, family, friends, I present to you Rosalinda Marie Montoya Fiore, daughter of King Alberto Almeida Montoya and heir to the throne of Costa Luna."

Rosalinda lifted the tiara off her head and held it in her hands.

"And then I say, 'She is willing to be your queen. If any person has a reason to object—'"

Whoosh! A gold-handled sword pierced the queen's crown, snatching it from the archbishop's now-trembling fingers, and pinned it to the carved wooden throne!

Rosalinda and Sophia gasped, and Rosalinda was shocked to see that the sword-thrower was none other than General Kane. Her tiara slipped from her hands and clattered to the ground.

"I object," General Kane proclaimed. "The *princesa* is too young to be queen. Costa Luna and Costa Estrella are two tiny countries who must unite and stand together against the world. Therefore, for the good of both our countries, I, General Magnus Kane, declare myself *el presidente de la República de las Costas*!" He spun toward the guards who hovered at the edges of the room. "Take them away!"

To Rosalinda's horror, Dimitri stepped away from her mother as a platoon of uniformed soldiers rushed into the courtyard to surround the staff. Two soldiers began striding directly toward her.

Rosalinda couldn't believe what was

happening. She was being overthrown before she'd even worn the queen's crown!

Then something even more unbelievable happened. A man came swinging down from the balcony on a rope. He barreled into the soldiers, knocking them to the ground in a heap. Then the man grabbed her. He whispered something to her mother that Rosalinda couldn't make out.

"Go with Major Mason," her mother told her, her tone deadly serious. "I will find you."

Rosalinda had never been so confused in her life.

"Go now!" her mother urged.

The fallen soldiers were back on their feet and rushing toward them. The man kicked them into the chocolate fountain and pulled Rosalinda in the opposite direction.

Rosalinda had no choice. She ran with the man who'd rescued her, who her mother seemed to trust, leaving the chaos, and her mother, behind.

They hurried down one of the palace's ornate

hallways. Rosalinda's heart was in her throat. What was going on?

"Who *are* you?" she asked, gasping for air as they ran.

"I'm here to protect you, Princess," Mr. Mason replied. "But you have to trust me."

"My mother," Rosalinda choked out. "What about my mother?" Ever since her father's death, Sophia had been both mother and friend. No one else mattered more to Rosalinda than she did.

"She's going to meet us. But we have to hurry."

Rosalinda and Mr. Mason flew through hallway after hallway and then ran down a darkly lit staircase. At its end Rosalinda saw her mother. She had never felt so relieved in her life.

"Are you all right, Mama?" she asked, fighting back tears as they embraced.

"Yes, my darling," Sophia assured her. "I knew General Kane would try something like this, so I made a plan to protect you." She tilted her head toward Mr. Mason. "You must trust Major Mason and do everything he says. Promise me you will do that?"

"Yes, Mama," Rosalinda said, nodding. "I promise."

She was just about to hug her mother again when they heard footsteps in the distance. General Kane's men were closing in on them. Mr. Mason told them they had to move now. They began walking quickly down a corridor.

"Mama, where are we going?" she asked, her mind whirling to think of where they could hide.

"Not we, *m'ija*. You. The general will say you abandoned your country. I must stay so the people know you will return when it is safe."

Rosalinda froze. She couldn't leave her mother! She wouldn't. "No! Not without you."

Sophia reached up and removed the gold locket around her neck and put it on Rosalinda. "No matter what happens, always remember you are a princess," she said quietly, her voice catching. "Do not worry, *reina bonita*. We will be together again soon."

They began to move once more and soon arrived at a large wooden door. As Mr. Mason opened the door, Rosalinda met her mother's gaze for a brief moment. Then Mr. Mason was pulling her over the threshold and slamming the door behind them.

As they ran through the palace's ornate gardens and out to the cobblestone streets of the city, Rosalinda's heart clenched with fear. Would she ever see her mother again?

*R*osalinda heard the *whop-whop* of a helicopter idling as she raced across a parking lot with Mr. Mason. When they reached the chopper, he lifted her inside. One of her beautiful shoes fell off in the process.

The helicopter roared into the air. She pressed her face to the glass, staring out at the land below. My kingdom, she thought, holding back a sob. She could make out her palace, and her mother, waving frantically from the balcony. She caught her mother's eye for just a second—and then the helicopter was flying quickly over the rain forest. Costa Luna was now nothing more than a dot in a sea of green.

$\mathcal{B}$ack at the palace, Sophia knew she had done the right thing, but it didn't make it hurt any less. She turned from the balcony to find the cold gaze of General Kane boring into her.

"You will never find her," she said defiantly. "And as long as she remains free, there will be hope in Costa Luna."

The general gave her a small, hard smile. "I could not agree more. But, the *princesa* is only a girl, madame. She will contact her mother. When she does, I will bring her back to Costa Luna, where she will rot with her mother in a tiny dirt cell."

Sophia stared back at him, fury swirling in her heart. She would not let him win.

Her country—and her daughter—depended on it.

Chapter

3

The helicopter landed on a remote desert island in the middle of the ocean. As Rosalinda climbed down with Mr. Mason and watched the chopper fly away, she felt a pang of trepidation. There goes my last chance at turning back for Costa Luna, she thought, trying not to panic.

She looked down at herself. Her beautiful coronation dress was covered with dirt, and the hem was ripped. She bent down and took off her remaining shoe, then stood back up. She lifted her chin. She was still a princess after all.

"What is this place?" she asked, gazing around at the trees.

"You'll see." Mr. Mason walked toward a cluster of heavy brush. To Rosalinda's amazement, a security door was concealed there. Mr. Mason placed his palm against a digital palm-reading pad.

"Major Joseph Mason," said a computerized voice. "Identity confirmed."

Following his lead, Rosalinda put her own hand on the pad. "Princess Number 379," the voice said, startling her. "Identity confirmed."

Rosalinda pulled her hand back. *Princess Number 379?* The door slid open to reveal a small, dark room.

"Where am I?" Rosalinda demanded. "Is this some kind of prison?"

"Not prison—" came a woman's voice.

And then a screen on the wall lit up, and there was the owner of the voice, a beautiful, professional woman wearing a suit.

"*Protection,*" she finished. "Princess Rosalinda

Marie Montoya Fiore, you are now in the safe custody of the P.P.P., the International Princess Protection Program."

Rosalinda sniffed. "I have never heard of it."

"Nobody ever hears about us until we're needed," the woman said calmly. "Good work, Major."

"Thank you, Director." Mr. Mason turned to Rosalinda. "You'll be safe now, Princess," he told her, and then he left the room.

Rosalinda remembered her mother's words. She must trust him. "How long am I staying here?" she asked the woman.

"Until you're ready for Stage Four," the Director replied.

"Stage Four?" she repeated. "What is Stage One?"

"Extraction. That's what brought you here."

This was starting to sound awfully intense. "And Stage Two?" Rosalinda prompted.

"Transition."

Rosalinda paused. "Transition to what?"

"Stage Three," the Director said. "Come inside, and I will explain everything."

The wall in front of Rosalinda opened to reveal a place like nowhere she had ever seen.

It was a massive room filled with people at computers talking into headsets as they worked. Everyone seemed to be busy typing and flipping through important-looking papers.

One entire wall was covered with a huge, flat screen. On the screen were several world maps, with electronic pointers zooming in on various countries. On another screen, girls' faces were flipping by quickly. Each girl was wearing a tiara and a beautiful gown. Rosalinda watched in awe.

"Welcome, Rosalinda, to the operational heart of the Princess Protection Program," the Director said, coming out to greet her. "A top secret agency funded by the world's royal families, we are actively providing protection services to twenty-nine princesses, all of whom have been threatened in one way or another."

The Director walked over to a computer

station, where a young woman was working. "Chloe, may I?"

"Of course, Director," Chloe replied. She scooted over, and the Director tapped a few keys on the keyboard.

Rosalinda stared at the monitor as a slide show of photos stopped on a princess in a beautiful silk sari with a sparkling diamond on her forehead. Servants fed her mangos and waved fans over her head.

"This is Princess Chandra," the Director said. "Last January, Major Mason rescued her from a politically motivated coup. We placed her where no one would find her." She tapped another key, and a different photo popped up. It was still Princess Chandra, but this time she sat in the middle of a frozen pond, wearing an unattractive hat with earflaps and a puffy, down coat. "Let's just say she's a little further north than she's used to."

Rosalinda gasped. "She is freezing!"

"Probably. But she's safe," the Director said.

"Chloe, report." The Director walked out of the room, followed by Chloe with a clipboard. Rosalinda hurried after them, taking a backward glance at the photo of the stunned Princess Chandra.

It was enough to make her shiver, too.

*R*osalinda knew it was bad manners to stare. But she had never seen anything like this. Ever. She rode down an escalator behind the Director and Chloe. Passing by them on the other side, going up, were three young women. They were dressed in regular clothes, but Rosalinda realized they were princesses. Each of them had an escort.

"Princess 383 has had a successful extraction," Chloe rattled off, checking her notes. "She arrives at oh-one-hundred hours. Princess 299 is still rejecting all attempts at transformation. Oh, and Princess 107 is in need of our services."

"Again?" The Director frowned. "She's gone through the program six times!"

Chloe sighed. "She says she has a stalker following her."

"She has a *bodyguard* and he's *paid* to follow her."

As they arrived at the bottom of the escalator, Rosalinda noticed a group of princesses wearing extravagant dresses. She wondered where they were going. More importantly, she wondered where *she* was going.

"What about me?" Rosalinda burst out. "Where are you sending me?"

"Nowhere yet," the Director told her. "First you will need to go through Stage Three. Transformation." They entered a gleaming, very modern, very busy hair salon. There were princesses of every shape and size being foiled, braided, weaved, and colored by a crew of hairdressers.

"First, we start with the hair," the Director said, guiding Rosalinda to the next area. "And then the wardrobe." Rosalinda saw several young women—princesses, of course, standing on small platforms in front of three-way mirrors. Seamstresses were measuring heights and lengths and holding up what looked like very regular clothes. None of the girls looked happy. There wasn't a sequin or jewel in sight.

"This goes on until you are unrecognizable as a princess," the Director said.

Before long Rosalinda was sitting in a salon chair and wearing a cotton robe. On it was the official P.P.P. logo. A hairdresser held a pair of scissors and lowered them toward Rosalinda's head.

"No!" she shrieked just as he was about to snip. "Stop!"

The hairdresser and Chloe looked shocked, but Rosalinda didn't care.

"I do not know any of you people!" she cried. "I want to speak with Major Mason. I only trust Major Mason."

He was her only hope.

"Take me back to my country," Rosalinda pleaded when Mr. Mason arrived. She paced back and forth in front of the mirror, her cotton robe swirling around her like a coronation gown. She couldn't stay here. She couldn't do this.

"Give me a minute here," Mr. Mason told the Director, who quietly stepped back.

He bent down and stared Rosalinda squarely in the eye. "Princess, I'm sorry, but General Kane has taken control of Costa Luna and assumed command of its government."

"But I have to go back!" Rosalinda protested, her thoughts racing to her mother and her kingdom.

"And you will," he assured her. "When we find a legal way to remove General Kane. Until then, you have to let us protect you."

"But what about my mother?" Rosalinda demanded. "Who is protecting her?"

Mr. Mason's answer surprised her. "You are," he said quietly. "As long as you're in Princess Protection, your mom will be safe. Kane is hoping you'll contact her so he'll know where to find you."

"And what if he does find me?" Rosalinda

asked, her voice barely above a whisper.

"He'll make an example of you by sending you to prison. Costa Luna will become his own personal kingdom with its true royal family a mere memory."

A tear slid down Rosalinda's cheek.

"Bottom line," Mr. Mason said soberly, "if you care about your country, if you care about your mother . . . nobody can know who you really are."

Rosalinda swallowed. How could she argue with that? Her family's future and legacy hung in the balance.

She walked regally back to the chair and sat down. "You may proceed," she announced.

The hairdresser gathered her long, dark hair in a low ponytail and . . . cut it off.

Rosalinda let out a small whimper as he placed the ponytail in her shaking hands. But she didn't cry.

Because, after all, she was a princess.

At least for now.

Chapter
4

*R*osalinda blinked in the bright sunlight, trying to take everything in. She had successfully completed Stage Three: transformation from princess to average American girl. Her long, dark hair was now shorter, with layers. Her glittering diamond bracelet and necklace were replaced with simple silver earrings. And her silks and satins had been traded in for blue jeans and a cotton top. But nothing had really prepared her for Stage Four. Relocation.

"Welcome to Louisiana, Rosie," Mr. Mason

said with a grin. He tossed a few freshly caught catfish into a bucket and headed to a building in front of them. JOE'S BAIT SHACK said a sign on top.

She followed him, making sure to avoid the bucket. Rosie. Rosie González, she thought, trying to make sure her new name sunk in. The Director at the Princess Protection Program headquarters had told her that she was no longer a princess. She was just a regular girl. And here she was, in a place General Kane would never think of looking for the princess of Costa Luna.

A bait shack in America.

What a day, Carter thought, slumping in her seat on the bus. Too many classes, too much homework, too many . . .

"Hey, looks like someone's home again," the bus driver, Helen, said as they pulled up to Carter's stop.

Carter looked up. Her dad's truck was parked in front of the Bait Shack. He was back!

"See you tomorrow!" she cried, grabbing her backpack and flying off the bus. She ran inside the Bait Shack. "Dad!"

But the place was empty. She ran outside and down the path to their house.

"Dad?" she called out, bursting through the front door. It wasn't a big place—just a kitchen-and-living-room combo, with two bedrooms and a narrow staircase leading to the bathroom on the top floor. Carter opened her bedroom door and tossed her backpack onto her bed.

"Hello," said a girl. She was sitting on the room's other bed.

"Hey," Carter said and walked back out.

What? Carter stopped in her tracks. There was a stranger. A girl. In her room.

Carter went back into the room. "Who are you?"

"Rosa . . . uh . . . Rosie?" said the girl.

"Are you sure? 'Cause you don't seem sure," Carter said.

"Yes," the girl said quickly. "Rosie. I am sure."

"So . . . what are you doing here?"

Rosie smiled. "Oh, Major Mason gave me this room."

Carter eyed her. "He did, huh?"

"Oh, yes," Rosie said, smiling even wider. "He's been lovely."

"Lovely?" Carter repeated.

Rosie nodded. "Of course, the suite is smaller than I am used to, but it will feel much larger when I have this extra bed removed."

"It's not extra," Carter snapped. "It's mine. Will you excuse me for a moment?"

Rosie gave a small nod.

Carter backed out of the room and shut the door. Her father had a lot of explaining to do.

She found him out on the old wooden pier, tying up a fishing boat.

"Hey, pal," he said as she strode toward him.

"Don't 'pal' me," Carter said, furious.

"Hmmm. So you met Rosie."

"Uh, yeah," Carter said. "Who is she and why is she in my room?"

Her dad sighed. "I had to bring her here. The Director didn't give me a choice."

For a moment, Carter had forgotten all about her dad's assignment. Now things were starting to add up. And she didn't like the math. "Oh, okay," Carter said slowly. "Because a *normal* dad would go off to a foreign country and bring his daughter a T-shirt, not a *person*!"

But it turned out that Rosie wasn't just a person. She was a princess. A princess in hiding, nonetheless.

"You should've warned me," Carter said, shaking her head in disbelief when her father finished his explanation.

"Carter, I didn't have a choice. She doesn't trust anybody but me."

"I know how she feels," Carter mumbled.

"Carter, what I do is complicated," her father said. "But if I thought for one second bringing her here would hurt our family—"

"Dad!" Carter burst out. But there was nothing more to say. Her dad had a job, and this

Rosie person was a part of it. "I get it!"

"So you're in?" Mr. Mason asked, cocking an eyebrow.

Carter shrugged. "Do I have a choice?"

"Good," he replied. "Because I'm going to need your help. She needs to stay here a while, undetected. And to do that, she needs to blend in. Like she's a normal American teenager."

Carter had figured out the undetected part. But that last bit? She had serious doubts. "Dad, she's not going to cut it," she insisted. "She's a princess." But her father's look told her that that type of thinking wasn't an option.

"Fine," she said. "Who do I say she is?"

Mr. Mason smiled. "Your cousin."

Carter snorted out a laugh. The whole thing was ridiculous. She was supposed to introduce the princess of Costa Luna as . . . her cousin?

"Thank you, Carter," her dad said. "If we do our job right, she'll be out of here and back to her own country before you know it."

"By Tuesday?" Carter asked hopefully.

Her dad smiled. "It'll be soon, I promise." He held out his fist. "It's still you and me, pal."

But Carter just let his fist hang there. She couldn't bring herself to do their secret hand-shake.

$\mathcal{I}$t was obvious that Carter Mason was not happy. Rosie could tell by the scowl on her pretty face—and the loud slam of the door when she stalked back into the cabin.

"You have made other sleeping arrangements?" Rosie asked politely.

"Look, the room's not *yours*," Carter said with a grimace. "We share it."

"Share?" Rosie repeated, bewildered.

"Share," Carter told her in a tight voice. "It means you get one side and I get the other. Stay on your own side."

And with that, Carter stormed back out the door.

Rosie stood there, shocked. No one had ever spoken like that to her before.

It appeared that life in Louisiana would be quite different than life in Costa Luna.

"So I thought princesses had designer clothes and everything," Carter said to her dad later that night. She tossed a card down on the table. She was a gin-rummy queen. Make that king. No, make that master. Nothing to do with royalty!

"She had to leave all that behind," Mr. Mason said, taking a bite of his pizza crust, then dropping the remnants in the box. "I thought you could loan her some of your stuff."

"Sure," Carter agreed, sarcasm oozing from her voice. "Why not?" She was sure she had *lots* of clothes a princess would want to wear.

"Thank you," her dad replied, ignoring her tone. "Now, go try again."

Carter shook her head. "After this hand."

"No. Now."

Carter slapped her cards down on the table. She went into the kitchen and grabbed a slice of pizza that was sitting on a plate and took it to her room.

"Kitchen's closing, last chance if you want to eat," she said to Rosie, who sat pouting on her bed.

"No, thank you," Rosie said primly. "I wish to sleep now."

Carter shrugged. "Okay." She turned to go.

"You may help me prepare for bed," Rosie called after her.

Carter turned slowly. "I may?"

"I need a nightgown. Preferably silk. Preferably pink."

Carter rubbed her chin thoughtfully. "Pink silk. Let me see." She walked over to her dresser and pulled out a pair of shorts, exactly like the ones she had on. "Here." She tossed them hard at Rosie, trying not to laugh as they smacked her in the face. It was obvious Rosie had never caught anything in her life.

"Por favor, dónde está el baño?"

Carter gaped at her. "Huh?"

"I would like to use your bathroom," Rosie translated.

"Upstairs. First door on the right."

"*Gracias.*"

"Okay. Whatever," Carter said, not even looking at her. She already missed the peace and quiet of her room. The sooner this was over, the better.

She and her dad were back at their game, when all of a sudden a scream sent shock waves through the cabin. Carter ran down the hallway, with her father right behind her. They looked up the stairs to see Rosie frozen in fear.

"What happened?" Mr. Mason demanded. "Did you see something?"

"Yes," Rosie replied. "I still see it."

Carter and her father looked around anxiously. With a shaking hand, Rosie pointed to a lizard crawling on one of the ceiling's pine beams.

"Oh, come on," Carter said, exasperated. She walked up the steps and let the lizard crawl onto her hand. "Don't they have lizards where you come from?"

"Maybe," Rosie answered. "But I never see them. That is why we have Henry."

"You have a royal reptile wrangler?" Carter asked, half-joking.

"Yes," Rosie said straight-faced. "And you should get one, too. Good night." Rosie walked stiffly down the stairs and back to the bedroom.

"She's going to be okay," Mr. Mason said, watching her go.

Carter shook her head. She'd been around enough nonroyal princesses to know that wasn't remotely possible with a real one. "No. She's going to be a royal pain."

Chapter
5

$\mathcal{R}$osie's first night's sleep in Louisiana had been fairly restful once she had pushed the lizard out of her mind and pulled the covers up to her chin. Now it was a beautiful sunny morning, and she sat waiting at the kitchen table for breakfast.

Unfortunately, no one was there to serve it to her.

She jumped as both bedroom doors opened, and Mr. Mason and Carter came into the kitchen. Rosie sat a little taller, patting her napkin in her lap.

"Good morning," she said.

Mr. Mason grunted a hello. He was busy opening cupboards, drawers, and the refrigerator, while Carter did the same thing. Rosie marveled that they didn't bump into each other once.

They sat down at the table on either side of Rosie with their breakfasts. She watched as Mr. Mason read his newspaper. To her horror, milk ran down his chin and he slurped his coffee. Even worse was Carter's loud chewing as she chomped through a doughnut.

It was then that Rosie realized they had no intention of getting breakfast for her. She cleared her throat.

Mr. Mason handed her a section of his paper. She took it, but she still wasn't sure what she was she supposed to do. Finally, he looked up at her.

"Don't be shy, Rosie," he said between swallows. "Grab whatever looks good."

Rosie looked over at the counter. Cereal

boxes, bread wrappers, a half-empty milk jug, and some doughnuts were spread over the counter.

Beeeeeeeeeep. A long honk came from outside the cabin.

Carter leaped up from the table. "That's the bus." She grabbed her backpack.

"Sure you don't want a ride?" her dad asked.

"No thanks." She turned to Rosie. "You coming?"

Rosie hesitated. "Where are we going?"

Carter gave her a look that made her feel as if she'd asked the silliest question in the world. "School. You're sixteen. You go to school." She handed Rosie a backpack.

"School. Of course." Rosie stood up and took the backpack. It was much heavier than it looked. She smiled.

Princess Rosalinda would be off to taste soufflés for her coronation or have a private Italian lesson or practice the piano. But Rosie González was going to high school.

*I*f Rosie is going to pass for a regular teen, she's not off to the best start, Carter thought as she walked past the Bait Shack and out to the waiting school bus.

"Hey, Helen," she said as she stepped onto the bus.

"Mornin' honey," Helen said, going to close the door. Then she stopped, her bright red lips forming an *O*. "Whoa. Who's this now?"

Carter turned. Rosie was running toward the bus, her backpack flopping left and right.

Carter grimaced. "Oh . . . that's my cousin."

Helen arched a heavily plucked eyebrow. "You don't say!" She held the door open and Rosie climbed on.

"Hello," Rosie said, gasping.

Helen looked at her. Carter rolled her eyes. Rosie had borrowed some of her clothes and made them look almost . . . princessy. She'd even tied a ribbon in her hair that looked vaguely like a tiara.

44

"Well, aren't you a cutie," Helen said appreciatively.

"I am Rosie," Rosie said, smiling.

"And I am late," Helen told her as she closed the door and put the bus in gear. The bus lurched forward, and Carter watched from her seat in the back as Rosie stumbled down the aisle. She shook her head. If Rosie could pull this off, she was definitely worthy of a crown.

*A*s the school bus bumped down the road, Mr. Mason stood in front of the Bait Shack, watching until it was a just a speck on the horizon. Then he went to his truck and pushed the button for the LCD screen. Soon he had established a link with the Princess Protection Program headquarters.

The Director's face appeared on the monitor. "What's your situation report?"

"Princess number 379 is in position. Stage Four is complete."

"She's safe then?" the Director asked.

"Affirmative. Absolutely safe." Mr. Mason turned off the screen and closed up the dash.

Then he started the truck and took off after the bus.

You could never be too sure.

*T*he moment Carter and Rosie got off the bus, a video camera was on them. But it wasn't the paparazzi. It was Ed, Lake Monroe's resident artsy video guy.

"Could this be the queen?" he asked, pushing the camera right in Carter's face.

She brushed past him. "Obviously not."

"Maybe this is the queen?" Ed asked, turning the lens on Rosie.

Rosie stopped, smiling. "Well, technically, no. Not yet, anyway."

"Nice," Ed said, nodding. "I like it. I'm Ed, by the way. And you're . . . ?"

"Rosie."

"Rosie, I'm making a documentary," Ed explained. "The rocky path from humble

46

peasant to homecoming queen."

"The queen of homecoming?" Rosie asked curiously. "What is this homecoming?"

Now Ed was the one to look puzzled. "You've never heard of homecoming?"

"No," Rosie said, shaking her head. "We have no such thing where I am from."

"Really? Where's that?"

Carter, who had continued toward the school, suddenly realized that while she had kept walking, Rosie had stopped—and was about to blab her true identity. She raced back and yanked on Rosie's arm. "Umm, Iowa," she told Ed. Then she pulled Rosie away. Under her breath, she hissed to Rosie, "What are you doing?"

"I do not understand," Rosie said, looking genuinely confused.

"You're supposed to act like a *normal* American girl," Carter reminded her. "You're supposed to just blend in."

"I am trying," Rosie insisted.

Carter narrowed her eyes. "Try harder." And this time when she walked off, Rosie was right on her heels.

*W*hile Rosie tried to learn the ropes at high school, her mother was standing before General Kane, refusing to help him.

"Any news from Rosalinda?" the general asked from where he sat at the king's desk, spinning a globe.

"No," Sophia said boldly. "And there never will be."

"Now, now, we must not be so negative," General Kane said soothingly. "Perhaps we should think happy thoughts, Sophia, eh? I am picturing a dashing young general, and he is sitting on a throne! Royal subjects shower him with adoration, and what do you know? They have crowned him their king."

"You will never be king of Costa Luna," Sophia burst out, enraged. "Not as long as I am alive."

"You're ruining my happy thoughts!" General Kane waved to Dimitri. "Take her away."

Sophia was led from the room. Oh, dear Rosalinda, she thought, filled with anxiety. I will stay strong. And you must do the same.

$\mathcal{T}$he crowds, the noise—Rosie wasn't sure where to look. She kept her eyes trained on Carter as they navigated down the hallway of Lake Monroe High School. But Carter knew where she was going and slipped quickly through the crowds. Soon Rosie was lost.

"Pardon," she said, tapping a student walking past. But he didn't stop.

"Your assistance, please," she called out to a girl who looked at Rosie, laughed, and continued on her way.

These people were most unhelpful. Rosie stood on tiptoe and made out the top of Carter's head as she walked into a classroom. Then she hurried after her.

When she walked inside the room, Rosie spotted an empty seat next to Carter. But before she could reach it, she saw Carter grab Ed's attention and motion for him to take the seat.

So Carter did not want her to sit there. That was fine, Rosie decided, lifting up her chin. There were plenty of other seats in the room. She would just need to ask someone to move out of one.

"May I take this seat?" she asked a boy seated near the front.

"Sorry. I think it's school property," he said, laughing and high-fiving his friend. Then he looked up at Rosie.

She smiled. The boy stared back at her.

"Yeah, uh, sure," he said, gathering up his books and moving to the back of the room.

Rosie took her seat as the teacher walked in. *"Bonjour, les étudiants."*

"Bonjour, Mademoiselle Devereux," the class responded.

"Comment allez-vous aujourd'hui?" Rosie

asked in perfectly accented French, oblivious to the stares around her.

The teacher looked quite pleased. "Ah, this must be our new student, Carter Mason's cousin."

Out of the corner of her eye, Rosie noticed everyone turn to look at Carter, who seemed to slide even lower in her seat.

"*Avez-vous étudié le français*, Rosie?" the teacher asked.

Rosie rested her arms on her desk and took a deep breath. "*Oui, j'aime le français. C'est une trés belle langue. Je parle six langues: l'anglais, le français, l'espagnol, le portugais, l'italien, et le japonais. Mais l'anglais est mon favorite . . . puisque je suis Americaine. Est-ce que cela vous a plus, vous, d'habiter aux Etas-Unis, Mademoiselle Devereux?*"

The French teacher beamed at her. "*Oui, merci*, Rosie."

Rosie smiled back. So far, high school was a breeze.

At lunchtime, Rosie stood in the doorway of the school cafeteria, scanning the room. Where could Carter be? Then she spotted her getting in line for food. Rosie made her way over and got in line behind Carter.

"Hey," a male voice complained. "Back of the line."

Rosie turned to see a big angry-looking guy. "Pardon me?"

"That's the rule," he barked, scowling. "No cutting."

Rosie was a bit taken aback. No one ever spoke to her like that in Costa Luna.

Then again, she never had to stand in line for her food. "Of course," she told him. "Then I will not cut."

"Hey, Rosie. Come on up with me!" It was the nice boy who had given her his seat in French class—Donny. She hurried up to join him.

"*Necesitamos más carne! Ahora!*" said a

dark-haired woman standing behind the counter.

Rosie perked up. She never expected so many opportunities to speak other languages here in Louisiana! *"Buenos días, señora."*

"Buenos días, señorita," the woman replied. And then, after several moments, added, "You gotta pick something."

"Oh!" Rosie said. She had assumed the woman would simply give her food. *"Muy bien."* She pointed. *"Qué es eso?"*

"Carne misteriosa," the woman whispered. Rosie gave her a blank stare. "Mystery meat."

Rosie wrinkled her nose, then pointed to a puffy-looking roll with some sort of flat disk of meat inside. "I'll have one of those. What is it?"

"A hamburger," the woman said, giving her a funny look.

"Gracias, señora. . ." Rosie started to thank her, but the woman was already on to the next person in line.

Rosie picked up her tray and started looking for a place to sit. Carter was already sitting at a crowded table, so she headed to an empty one and sat down by herself. She laid out a napkin for a place mat. Then she carefully placed her plate in the middle and set out her plastic cutlery. It was a far cry from a proper table setting, but it would have to do.

Rosie put another napkin on her lap, and then picked up her cutlery and began to cut her hamburger into bite-size portions.

Carter watched from her table as Rosie took bite after dainty bite of her hamburger with her fork. She rolled her eyes. Did the girl think she was eating filet mignon? To make matters worse, she realized that she wasn't the only one who had noticed. At the next table, Chelsea, Brooke, Donny, and his friend Bull were gaping at Rosie.

"Check her out," Chelsea said. "Who does she think she is?"

"Oh, I know!" Brooke said. "She thinks she's Carter's cousin."

Chelsea looked at Brooke and shook her head. But Carter noticed that Donny wasn't looking at either of them. He was smiling at Rosie. And she was smiling back at him.

Carter grabbed her tray, walked over to Rosie's table, and sat down across from her. "What are you doing?" she asked.

"Eating a hamburger," Rosie said, after swallowing one of her daintily cut pieces. "Have you ever tried one of these?"

"Of course," Carter said. Then she lowered her voice. "And, FYI, they have hamburgers in *Iowa*."

"Oh, right," Rosie said, and Carter detected a tiny blush.

"I thought you were going to blend in," Carter said accusingly.

Rosie's eyes widened. "I am blending."

"Speaking fluent French in class?" Carter scoffed. "Eating a hamburger like you're having tea with the queen?"

Rosie sat back. "How should it be eaten?"

Carter sighed. Did she have to do everything for this girl? She grabbed Rosie's hamburger, lifted the bun, and piled it with onions, lettuce, and pickles, adding a double squirt of ketchup and mustard at the end. Then she handed it back to Rosie.

"All right, grab it like this," she said, picking up her own burger. She waited patiently for Rosie to follow her lead. "Now, take a bite."

"Like this?" Rosie asked anxiously.

Carter sighed louder. Sure, Rosie was holding the burger with both hands instead of cutting it up with a knife and fork. But her pinkies were sticking up like she was holding a teacup.

"Stop," Carter instructed. She reached over and pushed down Rosie's pinkies.

Rosie adjusted her fingers and took a huge bite of the burger. And another. And another.

Carter smiled, satisfied with her pupil. Rosie's face is covered with every condiment possible, but at least she's got the technique down, Carter thought.

Just then the loudspeaker crackled to life. "Attention, please, students," came a man's voice.

Carter looked up. Principal Burkle had commandeered the lunch lady's microphone. And there was Ed with his camera, recording the whole thing.

"On Monday we will be taking nominations for your homecoming court," Principal Burkle announced. "These nominees must be girls of exemplary character—role models, if you will. Kind, intelligent, honest, charitable members of the Lake Monroe community. The three girls with the most votes will become your princesses."

The cafeteria broke into applause. Carter noticed many people looking over at Chelsea and Brooke, who smiled and waved to the crowd. She rolled her eyes. Of course they thought they would win. And even worse, they probably would.

"On Friday night one of these lucky girls will be crowned homecoming queen of Lake Monroe High," the principal finished.

Rosie pursed her lips. "You *vote* for royalty here?" she asked.

"We're a democracy," Carter told her. "We're into voting."

"So, anyone here can be a princess?" Rosie pressed. "Even you?"

Like that's going to happen, Carter thought. "Theoretically," she said glumly.

To her surprise, Rosie stood up. "May I have your attention?" she called out loudly.

"What are you doing?" Carter whispered frantically. "Sit down!"

But Rosie wasn't listening. "I would like to nominate my cousin Carter Mason to be your queen. I think she will make an excellent ruler."

Humiliation didn't cover the way Carter felt, as everyone in the cafeteria turned to stare at her. How could Rosie do such a thing? There was no way she would be chosen as one of the homecoming princesses.

Slowly, Carter stood up with her tray and walked out, her eyes never leaving the floor.

Chapter 6

"Carter!" Rosie called as the bus pulled away.

But Carter didn't stop. She hadn't spoken to her "cousin" the entire ride home. What had happened at lunchtime had caused enough mortification to last for her entire high school career.

"Carter—"

She stomped toward the house. "Leave me alone!"

Then Carter heard something that made her stop cold. "I order you to stop!" Rosie called out.

Carter spun around. "You *order* me? I order *you* to take a long walk off a short pier!"

Rosie put her hands on her hips. "You cannot order me to do anything!"

Carter laughed. "Wanna bet? You're in my kingdom now—"

"Whoa, whoa, whoa," Mr. Mason said, jogging over to them. "What's going on?"

Carter shook her head. "She can't do it, Dad. She can't act normal."

"I am normal," Rosie protested.

"Oh really?" Carter challenged. "So, a normal person has never seen a hamburger before, but can order one in six languages?"

Mr. Mason turned to look at Rosie, impressed. "Really? You did that?"

"I often speak to the staff in their native tongues," Rosie explained with a small shrug.

"See? Like that! They're not servants, they're lunch ladies." Carter turned to her father. "Can't you see this isn't gonna work?"

But her dad was not giving in. "Carter, it has

to work. We're in this together."

Carter stared at Rosie and her father. Rosie flashed a sweet, innocent smile.

Just great, Carter thought.

$\mathcal{T}$he next morning, Carter was hard at work in the Bait Shack, readying the store to open. All the boats were racked, the cash register was stocked with ones and fives, and the floor had been swept. There was just one more thing she had to do—until a blur of pink caught her eye.

"Great," Carter muttered. She watched as Rosie left the cabin and came running down to the Bait Shack.

"Good morning, Carter!" Rosie said as she walked into the shack. "What is it you are doing?"

"Ummm, Saturday chores." Carter said.

Rosie wrinkled her forehead. "Chores? I don't understand."

Carter shook her head. "Of course you don't."

"Perhaps I could learn this . . . chores. You

could teach me," Rosie said brightly.

Carter considered this for a moment. Then she said, "You know what? That's the first good idea you've had."

"What must I do?" Rosie asked eagerly.

Carter led Rosie over to two large containers that sat on the countertop. "It's easy. Your first chore—inventory."

"Inventory?" Rosie repeated.

"Counting," Carter explained. "You count what's in here"—she pointed to one container—"and put it in here." She pointed to the other. Then she headed for the door. "Have fun. Oh, and there's more on the shelf."

Carter tried not to laugh as she hurried out of the Bait Shack. "Hey," her dad said from where he stood putting some touch-up paint on a rowboat hull. "Everything okay?"

Carter grinned. "Just peachy."

How convenient that Rosie had arrived before Carter had finished her last chore: counting night crawlers.

* * *

They were wet. Slippery. Wiggly. And they are counted, Rosie thought as she dropped the last worm into its container. But when she turned, she saw shelves filled with more containers. They were too high to reach on foot, so she dragged over a ladder.

The ladder wobbled as she climbed up and reached for the shelf. Just as her fingers grazed one of the containers, the ladder tipped over. She screamed as she tumbled off and landed flat on the floor. She screamed again when the canister she'd almost had in her grip spilled bugs and worms all over her.

Carter and her father came running into the Bait Shack and stared. Rosie knew they had heard her scream. She also knew that she had made a mess of the newly cleaned shack. She climbed unsteadily to her feet and quietly headed for the door.

She would shower. She would put on clean clothes.

And she would find a way to make it up to Carter and Mr. Mason.

*H*ere they come, Rosie thought, looking out the window to see Carter and her father walking up to the cabin. They had spent all day cleaning up the Bait Shack. But still, they looked happy. They were laughing and talking, and Rosie smiled to herself in anticipation of what she had planned.

They came into the cabin, letting the screen door slam behind them. They stared at Rosie as they had earlier. However, this time Rosie smelled like vanilla, her hair was in a soft updo with flowers, and her smelly clothes had been replaced with a pretty dress that she'd found in the very back of Carter's closet.

The kitchen table was set for a formal dinner—at least as formal a dinner as she could plan without her royal staff. She'd found a white tablecloth and some linen napkins and the most beautiful china and silverware, too. Candles were lit, and classical music played low in the background.

"I didn't even know we still had all that stuff," Carter mumbled, taking it all in.

Her father looked speechless. "What's all this?"

"A proper dinner," Rosie said. "To thank you for cleaning up after the mess I made in your shop of bugs."

"It's bait," Carter corrected.

Mr. Mason went to pull out Rosie's chair, but she stopped him. "Thank you, Major, but tonight I serve you."

"All right, then," he said. "I won't say no to that. Carter, come on."

Carter wore a skeptical look as she took a seat at the table next to her father. "You cook?" she asked Rosie. "I thought you had servants for that."

"My mother grew up a peasant," Rosie explained. "She taught me a few family recipes." She carefully carried a large pot from the stove to the table. "*Arroz con pollo à la Fiore,*" she said proudly.

"Sounds too fancy," Carter said dismissively. "Let's just order a pizza—"

"It is chicken and rice," Rosie said, cutting her off.

"Fantastic! Bring it on!" Mr. Mason said enthusiastically.

Rosie ladled the steaming food into bowls. It smelled delicious. It smelled like home. Mr. Mason began to eat, and it made Rosie happy to see how much he was enjoying the meal. She had a sneaking suspicion that he had not had many home-cooked meals lately.

"Wow," Carter said, picking up a piece of bread. "Must be nice to play peasant for a day."

Rosie put down her spoon. She had wanted only to do something kind for Mr. Mason and Carter after everything they'd done for her. But it was clear to her now that Carter did not want any part of her. She turned to Mr. Mason. "Would you excuse me, please?" Then she stood up and ran to Carter's bedroom.

Carter knew that she hadn't exactly been welcoming to Rosie. But after all these years of it being just her and her dad, it was a little unsettling to have a third person living with them in the cabin. A person who was pretty and courteous and could cook *arroz con pollo*. A person her dad seemed to think was really nice.

A person who was a princess.

Carter's father was clearly disappointed in her behavior. And so here she was, standing awkwardly in her own bedroom, trying to make up for it.

Rosie was lying on her bed, staring up at the ceiling. "You do not know me, Carter."

"What's the big deal?" Carter blurted out. "You'll be back home with your servants and your personal chef and your private tutors soon enough."

Rosie was quiet. "How much did your father tell you about me?"

Carter shrugged. "Other than the obvious? We're on a need-to-know basis."

"I think you need to know," Rosie said soberly. "My real name is Rosalinda Marie Montoya Fiore and I am a royal princess. I am from a small island nation called Costa Luna."

"Never heard of it."

"It is not on most maps," Rosie continued. "It is very small, very unimportant to other large countries. But very important to me." She reached up to her neck and took off the locket she'd worn since she arrived. She handed it to Carter.

There was a small crest on the front. Inside were two tiny photos—a handsome man on one side and a beautiful woman on the other.

"When my father died, he left Costa Luna to me," Rosie explained.

"So, you're telling me you own a country," Carter said scornfully. But she felt a tiny pang of sympathy for this girl, so far from her family.

"I don't own it," Rosie clarified. "But I *am* responsible for it."

"You really don't need to—"

But Rosie wasn't about to be interrupted. "One month before my coronation, our palace was attacked. Your father was very brave. He—"

"Risked his life for you, I know," Carter cut in. "That's his job, to rescue poor, oppressed princesses."

"Did you know we had to leave my mother behind?" Rosie asked quietly. "The man who invaded Costa Luna now holds her as a hostage."

Carter shook her head, at a loss for words.

"They told me becoming Rosie González is the only way to keep her safe," Rosie continued, choking up.

"Stop," Carter said. She hated to see people cry—especially if she had anything to do with it. "It's okay."

"Carter, whatever I did to make you dislike me, I am truly sorry. I will try to do better. I will try to blend in . . . to be from Iowa. It's the only way I can save my mother's life."

"Let's just start over," Carter told her.

Rosie's face brightened. "Really? I would like that."

"But you have to lighten up on the princess stuff," Carter insisted. "It's really annoying."

Rosie gave a quick nod. "Absolutely. Please, I only want to be a typical American teenager."

Carter sat down on the bed next to her. "You know what? I think we can arrange that."

Chapter

7

*T*his is a most magical location, Rosie thought as she gazed around the huge space. She had no idea what it was, but there was music and the smell of fried food and loud crashing sounds. It was all so exciting. "I love this place!" she exclaimed to Carter. "What is it?"

"It's a bowling alley," Carter told her. She nodded toward long rows made of wood. "That is bowling. Just do what I do and don't draw any attention to yourself."

"Right," Rosie said, remembering her promise.

Less princess, more typical American teenager.

"Carter!" came a voice, and Rosie turned to see Ed walking over to them. He was a happy person, but when he saw Carter, he looked even happier.

"Hey, Ed," Carter said, sounding almost bored.

"Rosie, how you doing?" he asked.

"I am well, thank you," she said, smiling.

"What'll it be?"

"Bowling, please," Rosie said, feeling smart.

"No kidding." He laughed. "What size?"

Now Rosie didn't feel smart at all. "Excuse me?"

"Your feet," Ed said. "What size?"

Rosie hesitated. "I do not know," she whispered to Carter. "All of my shoes are made for me."

"There's a shock," Carter muttered. She looked over at Ed. "Just get her some shoes."

Ed darted off to get the shoes, and Carter walked away to choose a ball. Rosie sat on a stool, drinking in the colorful scene that was . . . bowling. A few moments later, Ed was back, holding out a pair of odd-looking shoes. Rosie held out her foot and Ed knelt down in front of her.

"Your Highness," Ed said, sliding a shoe onto her foot.

"Why, thank you, Edward," Rosie said.

"It's Edwin, actually," he corrected.

"Edwin," Rosie repeated. "That is a wonderful name."

He tied both of her shoes and helped her off her seat. "It's been a pleasure serving you, m'lady."

Rosie was in the middle of thanking him when she felt a hard tug on her arm.

"Excuse us, Romeo," Carter snapped as she pulled Rosie away. "You're not blending," she told her. "Pick a ball."

Rosie followed Carter over to a rack of bowling balls. They were large, black, and ugly. But next to them was a smaller rack with pretty, sparkly pink and orange balls. Much nicer! Rosie selected the pinkest one only to nearly drop it on her foot. It was much heavier than it looked!

"Careful there," Donny said. He took the

heavy ball from her hands. Rosie smiled.

She headed over to the lane Carter had selected with Donny following behind with her ball. But one look at Carter's face told Rosie she had done the wrong thing . . . again.

"You don't really have to do that, Donny," Carter said. "She can do it herself." She stared hard at Rosie. "Like a normal person. I'll just take it from here." She reached over and took the ball from Donny.

Rosie noticed that Donny wasn't even looking at Carter. "Whatever you say . . ." he said, leaving his sentence hanging.

"Carter," Carter said. Rosie was taken aback. Surely Donny knew her name!

He nodded. "Right." He headed back to his friends, flexing his muscles. Rosie found this quite unappealing. But from the look on Carter's face, Rosie knew her friend felt differently.

"Is Donny your boyfriend?" Rosie asked.

Carter flushed. "What? No! He's just a friend."

Rosie wasn't sure that was really the truth. "But he is special to you," she pointed out. "I see the way you look at him. It is the same way Ed looks at you."

A funny look passed over Carter's face. "Okay, you're obviously not from here. Just . . . bowl. You first."

"Good. How do I win?"

Carter explained that the goal was to knock down all the white pins. Then, she dumped the pink bowling ball into Rosie's hands.

In the next lane, Chelsea was bowling. Rosie watched as she gracefully stepped forward and sent the ball sailing down the lane. Rosie looked down at her own lane. Then she swung her ball back, but it was so heavy that its weight spun her around so that she was facing the back of the alley. Rosie's hand came flying down with the momentum of the ball's weight. The ball dropped to the floor, sailed through her legs toward the pins and . . . *strike*!

Rosie spun around to see that she had

knocked down every pin! Donny and his friends were clapping and whistling. So she did what came naturally.

She curtsied.

$\mathcal{C}$arter was glad that Rosie was having fun, but her enthusiasm for bowling was getting a little tiresome. She decided to call it a night.

"You done already, Carter?" Ed asked as she placed the rented bowling shoes on the counter.

"Our lane's getting a little crowded," she muttered. She glanced back at Rosie, who was laughing and bowling with Donny, Chelsea, and Brooke.

Ed took the shoes. "You don't really like your cousin, do you?"

"Oh, no," Carter said quickly. "It's just she's kind of, you know, a—"

A princess. Not that she could say that. But she was. And not only was Rosie a real princess, she might even be chosen as a homecoming princess at school. The vote was on Monday.

And at this rate, Carter thought, watching her talk and laugh with Chelsea, Brooke, and Donny, she was well on her way.

"I must be a natural bowler," Rosie said happily, plumping her pillow. She had had a wonderful time at the bowling alley.

"It's called beginner's luck," Carter said from her bed. She rolled onto her side, facing the wall.

"Chelsea and Brooke were very nice to me," Rosie went on. The girls had even come up with a nickname for her: Ro. It seemed like she was fitting in here in Louisiana after all. She glanced over at Carter.

"Carter?"

"What?"

"Why do you care so much for that boy Donny?"

Carter paused for a moment before responding, "Who says I care for him?"

Rosie was silent. Carter's feelings were quite obvious.

"Okay, fine," Carter blurted out. "I've been totally in love with him since third grade when he kissed me under the basketball hoop. Is that what you want to hear?"

"He is quite beautiful," Rosie agreed. "Much like a prince." She played with the fringe of her blanket. "I wonder if he is beautiful on the inside as well." Then she yawned. "Shall we bowl again tomorrow?"

"I can't," Carter told her. "I have to work at the Bait Shack."

"I have never worked before," Rosie said thoughtfully. "It is normal to do this?"

"Yeah," Carter replied. "Lots of kids have jobs."

"Then I will help you," Rosie announced.

"You can't," Carter said.

"Why not?"

Carter rolled over. "Because it's *my* job, and you can't have everything that's mine! If you want a job so bad, go get your own." And then she rolled back to face the wall again.

* * *

$\mathcal{L}$ifting live bait traps from the water was nothing new for Carter. But being filmed while doing so was.

"Ed!" she screeched as he stuck his camera right in her face.

"Here she is, folks, a future homecoming princess of Lake Monroe, Louisiana. Who is this natural beauty, you ask?"

Ignoring him, Carter walked off the pier and toward the Bait Shack, the trap swinging alongside her.

"Go away," she said. "I'm working."

But Ed wouldn't be stopped. "This is Carter Mason. Secret identity? Bait Girl. So confident of her innate royalty, she's unafraid to handle whatever disgusting creature—"

He stopped then, but only because Carter was shoving a trap full of wriggling crawfish right at the lens.

"Hey! Not on the camera!" he protested, wiping the lens with his shirt.

Carter grinned. "Well, turn it off."

"No. Today's my last day to get the 'before' footage. The vote is tomorrow."

Carter scuffed her sneaker on the grass. "Well, go shoot Chelsea or Brooke."

"Nah," Ed said. "I've got tons of them already. They pay me to film them."

"Is that why you're doing this?" Carter asked. "For the money?"

He nodded. "Absolutely. I'm the only senior who doesn't have a car. This little film is gonna make me some paper." Carter could feel his eyes on her. "You really hate this whole princess thing, don't you?"

"I don't hate it exactly," she said. "I think it's shallow. Girls like Chelsea and Brooke, all they think about is *shoes*, like wearing the right clothes makes them all superior. I just want to do something more important with my life. Like my dad."

He smiled. "Yeah, he does sell some sick bait."

Oops, Carter thought. Way to almost spill her dad's secret. No one knew that Mr. Mason really *did* have a secret identity.

"Speaking of princesses, where's Rosie?" Ed quipped.

Carter shrugged. "How should I know?"

And then Ed's cell phone beeped. "Text message," he said, looking at the display. "And I think I just found her."

Chapter 8

$\mathcal{R}$osie looked down at the cow logo on her shirt. She hadn't expected to find a job so easily, yet here she was, a new employee of Udderly Yogurt.

"Thank you for giving me this job," she told Chelsea. Her new friend was giving her a tour of the shop.

"No prob, Ro," Chelsea said. "Daddy owns, like, seventeen Udderlys all over the South. He's the king."

Rosie gasped. "Your father is a king?"

Chelsea nodded. "Of frozen yogurt. Oh, one more thing." She handed Rosie a visor with a cow on it. "You have to wear this."

Chelsea turned to three big stainless-steel machines. "So this is a frozen-yogurt machine. You just pull this lever, and when it comes out you put a little swirl on top, and you're good to go, okay?"

Rosie looked at the machines, then back at Chelsea. "I do not understand."

"Oh, don't worry, Ro," Chelsea said. "You'll get the hang of it. And all your friends will be here to support you. We really want you to succeed at your first job."

Rosie smiled. "That is very nice. Thank you."

Chelsea flashed her a grin. "No prob." Then she was out the door. She flipped the shop's CLOSED sign to OPEN on her way.

Surely this couldn't be too complicated a job, Rosie thought. If it were, Chelsea would never have left her all alone in the shop. She picked up a cone and pulled the lever.

Whoosh. The yogurt came gushing out of the machine, overflowing the cone and plopping onto her shoe. Frowning, she stepped back and tried again.

And again.

And again.

Each cone was worse than the one before. Cones that leaned to the side. Cones that spilled onto her hands. Cones that leaked at the bottom. And as for the swirl? Forget it.

Suddenly, Rosie realized that the shop was filling up. It seemed like all of Lake Monroe High School was in line to get some frozen yogurt.

Wiping her hands on a paper towel, Rosie took an empty cone from a stack and tried again. And finally, practice made perfect. *I'm even getting the swirl!* she thought excitedly as she flicked her wrist at just the right moment. The swirl looked exactly like the one on the giant frozen yogurt sign behind her. Grinning, Rosie was moving the handle to stop the flow of yogurt when . . . *guuuuusssssshhhh*. Frozen yogurt started pouring out of the machine. "No!" she cried, trying to stop it, but the handle wouldn't move.

Frantic, Rosie looked around Udderly Yogurt for someone to help her. Her eyes scanned the crowd and had just landed on Carter when *whoosh!* Rosie's feet slipped from under her and she fell hard on the floor in a pool of melting yogurt.

Everyone began laughing. Seconds later, Carter was there with Ed, pulling her to her feet.

"What are you doing here?" Carter asked.

"You said to get a job!" Rosie cried, wiping a blob of yogurt off her cheek.

"Not this job!" Carter was fuming. "This job is for losers. Trust me, I used to work here. The bait gig is a step up."

Ed tilted his head. "Check it out."

Rosie followed his gaze past all the laughing students over to one of the tables, where Chelsea and Brooke sat. The girls waved.

"What is happening?" Rosie asked slowly.

"Chelsea set you up," Carter said hotly. "She invited all these people just to watch you make a fool of yourself."

At this, Rosie reached out to touch Carter's shoulders. "Carter, it's okay. I am not a fool." She resolutely straightened her visor. "She cannot make something of me that I am not."

"We can't let them get away with this," Carter said.

"I will turn the other cheek," Rosie said. "That is what princesses do." And with that, she removed the visor and walked to the front of the shop, making sure not to slip in the melting mess.

When she reached Chelsea, she handed her the visor. "Your father, the king of yogurt, would be very disappointed in you, Chelsea." Rosie had believed that Chelsea was her friend. But she knew that no true friend would ever behave this way.

Rosie walked out of the shop. She thought Carter was right behind her—and she was—except that Carter had first stopped to dump a sundae on an unsuspecting Bull.

"Sorry, but I'm not a princess," Carter said, looking over at Rosie as Bull stormed off to get some napkins.

And even though she was covered with yogurt, Rosie had to laugh. Carter Mason was not a princess. But she was a royally good friend.

$\mathcal{B}$ack at Udderly Yogurt, Chelsea was not happy. All around her people were talking about Rosie—how cool and sweet she was, and how she'd make a great homecoming princess. It was more than she could bear. She was just about to lay into an unsuspecting freshman who said he would vote for her when Brooke pulled her away.

"You're losing it, Chels," Brooke cautioned.

But Chelsea could not be calmed. "Did you hear that? She can't be a princess!"

Brooke grimaced. "Um, don't freak or anything, but she kinda can." She held up her cell phone. "I've just been texted, like, ten times. Everybody thinks she's pretty cool. Tomorrow, when the whole school votes for the three princesses, she could be one of them. And if she gets enough votes—"

"Don't say it," Chelsea hissed.

"She could become queen," Brooke finished.

"No, *I'm* the queen!" Chelsea practically shouted. "It's my destiny!"

By now everyone in the shop was looking at them. "Mmm, that's iffy," Brooke said.

"I'd rather eat carbs than see her wearing my crown. We have to stop her!"

"How?" Brooke asked.

"If she never becomes a princess, she can't be the queen, right?" Chelsea said.

"I'm not sure where you're going here . . ." Brooke started to say. But by then Chelsea had grabbed her phone and was pushing its buttons in a frenzy.

"Get another phone," Chelsea barked. "We've got a whole lot of texting to do."

Chapter 9

The flaming orange sun was just hitting the tops of the trees on its way down as Carter leaned back, staring out at the water. This was her favorite time of day. And for once, she was sharing it with a friend.

"It's a skill most Americans master in the third grade, but it's never too late to learn," she was telling Rosie.

"I am ready to try," Rosie said. She opened her can of soda, guzzled, and then . . . *burppppp.*

"Nice," Carter said, laughing. "Next we'll

work on slouching, eye rolling, and talking back to my dad."

Carter could hardly believe she was hanging out on her fishing pier with a real princess. But the more she got to know Rosie, the more she was starting to see that beneath the dresses and jewels Rosie was a regular person after all.

"If Mr. Elegante could see me now, he would be so mad," Rosie said, shaking her head at the thought.

"Who's Mr. Elegante?"

Rosie smiled. "My royal dress designer."

"You're kidding, right?"

"No. He is a wonderful friend to our family. If there were ever an emergency, he's the one I would call."

"Your own designer," Carter mused. "Must be nice to be queen."

"It's not all about dresses and crowns, Carter," Rosie assured her new friend. "My mother told me my father never called himself king. To our people, he was father, brother, and friend." She gazed out at the horizon. "I hope to be like him when I am queen of Costa Luna. I want to make a difference."

Carter knew how she felt. "To do something important with your life?"

"Yes," Rosie said with confidence.

"You're different than I thought a princess would be," Carter confessed, swinging her legs back and forth over the water.

"I hope that is a good thing."

Carter nodded. "Yeah. That's a good thing."

Rosie looked over at her. "Thank you for helping me today. A princess is never sure who is a true friend. Today I am sure."

Carter gave her a genuine smile. "Me, too." Then they both took a big swig of soda—and belched in unison.

$\mathcal{B}$ack in Costa Luna, the palace was still in turmoil. General Kane was in the king's office, looking at a display case of military medals. "I'll give myself this one and this one," he said, selecting two. "For bravery and honor."

"A thief has no honor," Sophia declared as she was escorted into the room by a soldier.

The general turned to greet her. "Sophia! Come in, come in—we have a great deal to discuss." He gazed into the mirror and pinned the medals to his coat. "Do you think it's too much? I want to look my best when I announce my engagement."

"You're getting married?" Sophia asked. "Who could be so unfortunate as to be your bride?"

Kane smiled. "Well, as a matter of fact, she is standing right here in this room."

He meant her? Sophia gasped. "That is ridiculous. I will *never* marry you."

"Of course you won't," Kane said as if speaking to a child. "But Rosalinda will not know this." A chill came over Sophia's heart as he went on. "She will see the announcement, assume you are doing it to protect her, and come racing back to her mother's side, just in time to join you in exile."

Sophia was defiant. "The people of Costa Luna will never accept this."

"The same was said for the people of Costa Estrella twenty years ago," General Kane reminded her. "And look what happened." He turned to Dimitri the guardsman. "Take her back to her cell."

There was a buzz in the air as Carter and Rosie walked through the school's front doors Monday morning. Everyone seemed to be racing to get somewhere.

"Good morning, students," came Principal Burkle's voice over the loudspeaker. "The votes for your three homecoming princesses have been tabulated. And now, I'd like to announce the winners."

Rosie pulled Carter down the hall into the jam-packed cafeteria just as the announcement was being read.

"Your princesses are . . . Chelsea Barnes!" Principal Burkle said. Chelsea ran up beside him, blowing kisses to the crowd. Mademoiselle Devereux held three crowns on top of a velvet pillow. She placed one on Chelsea's head.

"Carter Mason!" the principal continued.

Carter froze. Was she hearing things? Apparently not, because Rosie threw her arms around her while her French teacher placed a crown on her head. Weirdest of all was that Chelsea and Brooke were actually applauding for her.

"And your third and final princess is . . . Rosie González!"

The crowd went nuts, and Carter watched as Rosie accepted her applause. It's like she's back home at her palace, she thought as Rosie gave the student body a regal wave. Carter grabbed her by the wrist and hurried her over to the side of the room.

"This isn't good," she whispered. "Me being a princess is not normal."

A guy's voice interrupted their conversation. "Hey, there." Rosie spun around and was suddenly face to face with Donny.

Carter is bummed when Donny gives Chelsea
and Brooke a ride to school instead of her.

Princess Rosalinda prepares for her coronation
rehearsal as her mother, Sophia, looks on proudly.

Major Mason leads Rosalinda to the helicopter,
which will take them to P.P.P. headquarters.

Rosalinda is unhappy to learn that she cannot return
to her country, and her mother, until it is safe.

"She can't act normal, Dad," Carter said. "Can't you see this isn't going to work?"

Rosie counts night crawlers at the Bait Shack.

"Carter, whatever I did to make you dislike me, I am truly sorry," Rosalinda said. "I will try to do better."

Carter teaches Rosie how to be a typical American teen by taking her bowling.

"Thank you for giving me this job, Chelsea,"
Rosie said on her first day at the yogurt shop.

"You're different than I thought a princess would be,"
Carter told her new friend with a smile.

Carter tries on dresses for the homecoming dance at the thrift shop.

Brooke shares the article she found—which reveals Rosie's true identity—with Chelsea.

Rosie shows Carter the magazine Chelsea brought over.
"I have to leave, Carter," she said.

Carter tries on her mask for the homecoming dance,
hoping her plan goes off without a hitch.

"You deserve better than him," Rosie told Carter after Carter turned Donny down.

Queen Rosalinda smiles at her royal subjects after her coronation ceremony.

"Uh, Rosie, can I talk to you?" he asked. Carter noticed that, for once, he seemed almost shy.

"Me?" Rosie asked.

Donny shuffled his feet. "Yeah, um, you know there's the homecoming dance and everything, and now that you're a princess . . . will you . . . will you go with me?"

"Me?" Rosie said again.

"Her?" Carter managed to get out.

Donny nodded. "Yeah. I want you to be my date for the dance."

Rosie touched his arm. "Oh, Donny. That is very sweet of you—"

Carter could not believe this was happening. Feeling the threat of serious tears, she ran to the cafeteria doors.

Rosie gave Donny an apologetic look and then finished, "—but no. Will you excuse me, please?"

"Uh, sure," Donny said, looking baffled.

By the time the school day ended, Rosie had

managed to find Carter and clear up any misunderstanding. But that didn't make Carter feel much better. When they got home from school, she headed straight for the Bait Shack.

"That was the most humiliating thing that's ever happened to me," she said, taking off the crown and yanking her Bait Shack hat off its hook. "And I've been humiliated a lot." She pulled the old hat on her head. "What was I thinking? A guy like Donny would never go out with me." Carter squeezed her eyes shut, but the humiliating moment of his asking Rosie to the dance right in front of her was seared into her brain forever.

"Then he is not worthy of you," Rosie insisted, crossing her arms.

"You can say that because you're all high and royal," Carter said. "But I'm just a girl who sells worms."

Rosie's eyes blazed. "No, you are so much more! You are a princess now!"

Carter laughed. "Trust me. I'm *not* a princess."

"Yes you are." Rosie was adamant. "You just do not feel like one yet."

What Carter felt like was erasing this entire day. She tried to walk out of the Bait Shack, but Rosie blocked her way. "When I came here, you taught me how to act normal, not royal. Now it is my turn to teach you. You think being a princess is superficial."

"I guess," Carter admitted.

"You think it is about what you wear, how you look . . . well, it is a little bit about how you look." Rosie plucked the Bait Shack hat off Carter's head and circled her with a critical eye, pushing back her shoulders, lifting her chin, removing the ponytail holder from her hair. "But mostly it is what you have to offer the world and who you are inside." She gave Carter a wide grin and put the crown back on her head. "C'mon Carter. Let's find your inner princess."

Chapter 10

The rest of the week was a whirlwind of activity. Carter and Rosie set up a table at school and offered free tutoring to anyone who wanted it—Rosie in foreign languages, Carter in math and science. They went to the library where Rosie read fairy tales to a captivated preschool audience. And they cleaned out the cabin and brought all the old clothes, dusty books, and gently used appliances to a thrift shop where the proceeds would be given to the needy.

"You're just so good with everybody," Carter said enviously. She was wearing a vintage dress that she'd found at the thrift shop and was walking across her bedroom, balancing a book on her head. "Kids, old people . . . you're probably even great with dogs."

"Yes, that is true," Rosie agreed.

Carter sighed. Her assumption that princesses were spoiled brats, well, it didn't hold up anymore. "You're just so much more generous than I thought you'd be."

"At home, it's my job to help people," Rosie explained.

"I guess I never really thought about what it means to be a princess," Carter said. She gazed upward. "Like this. I can't believe you actually have to do this."

"Oh, I don't," Rosie said smiling.

Carter yanked the book from her head. "Then why am I doing it?"

"Because it is funny." She giggled.

"I hate you," Carter said, mock stone-faced.

Rosie looked aghast. "You do?"

Carter started laughing "Oh, I didn't mean it that way. I didn't mean, 'I hate you, I hate you.' I meant . . . 'I hate you' like you're my best friend."

Rosie lit up. "Oh. Then I hate you, too. And that dress is ugly."

Carter's eyes widened. "It is?"

Rosie shook her head, laughing at her failed attempt at a joke. "No. It is beautiful. And so are you. Look." She pulled Carter in front of the mirror and placed her princess crown on her head. "You are becoming a princess on the inside. Now you look like one, too."

Carter gazed at her reflection in the mirror. Rosie's right, she realized. I'm . . . I'm a princess.

*H*anging out in the library wasn't exactly a habit for Brooke. She walked up to the school librarian. "Excuse me, I have this lame reading assignment for Spanish class. Do you have anything that's really easy . . . with lots of pictures?"

The librarian stared at her for a moment,

then put a stack of glossy magazines on the counter.

"Oooh," Brooke said. "Cool." Scooping up the magazines, she found a table and sat down.

But she found something that made studying impossible. There, on the page in front of her, was a picture of Rosie González and her mother. Under Rosie's picture there was a caption. A caption that said she was a princess!

"*Princess* Rosalinda?" Brooke whispered, her mouth dropping open. *"No way."*

$\mathcal{M}$r. Mason was carrying buckets into the Bait Shack when he heard his cell ring. He put down the buckets and headed to his truck, punching the buttons on the dash as he slipped on his headset. Up popped the LCD screen—and on it, a split-screen photo. On one side, the cover of a Spanish gossip magazine. On the other, a photo captioned: "Princess Rosalinda Montoya Fiore of Costa Luna."

"It's Mason," he said into the headset. "What's going on?"

"General Kane's announcement of his engagement to Doña Sophia Montoya has popped up in a sleazy gossip magazine," the Director said. "So far, we've been able to contain the story, but I'd be lying if I said I wasn't concerned."

Mr. Mason scrolled to the next image on the screen—a photo of the princess and her mother. The caption read, "Royal Mother to marry General Kane of Costa Estrella."

"She'd never agree to marry that jerk," Mr. Mason scoffed.

"I'm not suggesting that she would, Major."

"General Kane's doing this to draw Rosalinda out," he replied, thinking aloud.

The Director agreed. They would have to keep this news from Rosalinda. Her safety depended on it.

"Major, has she made any enemies?" the

Director asked. "Anyone who would want to expose her identity?"

Mr. Mason couldn't think of a single one.

$\mathcal{T}$here was still so much decorating to be done for the homecoming dance the next night. Chelsea strode through the school gym, her head swiveling. Lots of balloons, the queen's throne with its velvet cushion . . .

"Let's move that throne here," Chelsea said. She pointed to the middle of the dance floor. A girl named Margaret scurried behind her taking detailed notes. "And let's have a few more of those lights directly on it. We should bring in a lighting designer."

"The budget's gone, Chelsea," Margaret said. She hovered nervously near Chelsea, clutching a clipboard. "What you see is what you get—"

"Okay, okay." Chelsea cut her off. Then she gasped. "I know! A follow spot just on me. Maybe soft pink—or golden, like the sun!" She let out a contented sigh. "It's good to be queen."

"Uh . . . you're not queen yet," Margaret said.

"Can it, Muffy," Chelsea snapped. She saw Brooke walk in then.

"Hey, Chels," Brooke said.

"Don't call me that," Chelsea said, frowning. "You lost that right when you lost your princess crown to Bait Girl and her cousin."

Brooke raised an eyebrow. "What if we could get Rosie to drop out of homecoming altogether?"

"She would never do that."

"She might." Brooke handed Chelsea a copy she'd made of the magazine page. "She's not who she says she is. She's *Princess Rosalinda*."

Chelsea stared at the photo. "What does the article say?"

"Um . . . ," Brooke said. She hadn't even realized there *was* an article. She took back the paper and began to read. "It's about Rosie and her mother. One of them has fled the country and one of them is in prison . . . or a paper bag. I get those two mixed up."

Chelsea squeezed her arm. "No biggie. Good job, Brookie."

Brooke grinned. "Thanks, Chels."

*M*eanwhile, in Carter's bedroom, Rosie was hanging her homecoming dress next to Carter's in the closet, smoothing out any wrinkles. She was looking forward to dressing up again after weeks of wearing jeans and T-shirts. And then a voice came from the hallway.

"Podemos entrar, Princesa Rosalinda?"

"Si, entren por favor—" answered Rosie without missing a beat. And then, horrified, she spun around. When she had heard someone asking permission in Spanish to enter the room, she'd replied without thinking. But for someone to have addressed her in Spanish, using her real name . . .

Chelsea and Brooke were standing in the doorway.

"I've never heard of Costa Luna, have you, Brookie?" Chelsea asked, not taking her eyes off Rosie for a second.

"No, Chels," Brooke replied, grinning.

"I do not know what you are talking about." Rosie tried to cover, but she knew it was no use. They had discovered who she was.

"Drop the act, Ro," Chelsea said, her eyes narrowing.

Brooke crossed her arms. "We know all about you and your mother . . . and the paper bag."

"What?" Rosie asked, confused.

Chelsea dropped a piece of paper on the bed. There were photos of her and her mother, along with an article.

"Poor Princess Rosalinda," Chelsea said with a sneer. "Have you heard she's in hiding?"

I need Carter, Rosie thought. Her friend was out on the pier hauling in minnow traps. "You do not understand," she said. "I—"

"We understand you lied to us," Chelsea said tartly.

Rosie shook her head. These girls had no

idea what potential tragedy they could cause. "Only to protect my mother!"

"From the paper bag?" Brooke asked meaningfully.

Rosie didn't understand Brooke's comment, but she did understand how serious this situation was. "Look, I will give you a reward for keeping my secret," she told them.

"Oh, we know you will," Chelsea said.

Rosie blinked in surprise. "You do?"

"Yes, and we already have it picked out," Chelsea told her.

Rosie had a feeling that it wasn't going to be that easy. "I don't understand."

Brooke looked twice as confused. "Uh, yeah, me either."

Chelsea's voice was cold as ice. "You're turning in your crown, Princess. You're going to tell everyone that there is and can only ever be one true homecoming queen, and that's me."

Brooke's eyes widened. "Oooh, that's good."

"Fine," Rosie agreed. "You can have my crown,

but not Carter's." She thought of her friend's excitement back at the thrift shop when they'd each found the perfect dress. She could not let that happiness be taken away from her. "She is no threat to you, Chelsea," she said gently.

Chelsea sniffed. "Oh, fine. Let Bait Girl play princess for one night." Then she walked over to the vintage dresses, giving them the once-over. "She just won't look like one."

Carter walked up to the cabin from the pier, her feet making a squelching noise in her water-logged sneakers. Mud had caked on her shins, and she couldn't wait to hop into the shower.

To her surprise, she saw Brooke's car pulling away from the cabin. If they were around, something bad had to be happening.

Carter's eyes met Chelsea's, and she watched, horrified, as Chelsea tossed two dresses out of the car. They landed in a huge mud puddle. Carter ran and picked them up. Her dress for the dance—and Rosie's—were now soggy, ruined messes.

Carter stormed into the cabin to her room, the muddy dresses in her arms. "Look what Chelsea and Brooke just did!" she exploded. "I can't believe them!" She paused when she saw Rosie sitting on the bed, her face blotchy. It was obvious she had been crying. "What's wrong?"

Rosie looked at her through red, teary eyes. "I have to leave, Carter."

"Leave?" Carter asked. "Leave where?"

"Back to my country." Rosie handed Carter a piece of paper.

It was a photocopy of a magazine article. Carter read about Rosie's mother's engagement to General Kane. It's the guy Rosie told me about, Carter realized. The one who invaded Costa Luna.

"Would your mother really marry this General Kane loser?" Carter was doubtful. From what Rosie had told her, Sophia was an intelligent woman. She wouldn't pick someone like the general for a husband.

"To protect me from him, my mother will do whatever she has to."

"My father is never going to let you go back there," Carter told her. And it was the truth. Mr. Mason would never let Rosie put herself in harm's way.

"He'll never know."

"Well, I know," Carter retorted. "And I'm not letting you, either."

"Carter, you have to stay out of this. I have a duty to my people. This is something you can never understand." Her voice softened. "I have loved living in Louisiana. I wish my life could always be like this. But this is not reality. You think my life as a princess is a fairy tale? This life, here, this is a fairy tale! I cannot hide here anymore."

As much as she didn't want to believe that, Carter knew Rosie was right. She couldn't go on having a "cousin from Iowa" forever.

"Soon I will be queen of Costa Luna," Rosie said tearfully. "My country needs me."

Carter drew in a deep breath. "You're right. They *do* need you. They need you to lead them, to protect them, something you can't do from jail—which is exactly where you'll be if you go back to Costa Luna."

Rosie stood up, tears streaming down her face. She hurried from the room, leaving Carter alone.

"No way I'm letting this happen," Carter said aloud to herself. She would come up with a plan that would protect not only Rosie, but Sophia and Costa Luna, too.

Chapter 11

"*Hola*, this is Elegante!" Señor Elegante said into his cell phone. He did not recognize the voice on the other end. And the person would not identify herself when he asked her to.

Because it was Carter Mason.

"All that matters is that I'm a friend of Princess Rosalinda, and she's about to make a big mistake." Carter hurried to get it all out. Rosie had said that Elegante was a trusted friend. She hoped she could trust him now.

"My *princesa*?" Elegante sounded surprised. "What mistake is this?"

"She wants to come home," Carter explained.

"Oh, no, she must not do that. It's too dangerous!"

And with those words Carter knew that she could trust him one hundred percent. "I know," she whispered. "But I have a plan. I need you to listen very carefully."

"I will do anything for the *princesa*. Anything."

Then Carter told him what she had in mind.

*L*ater that day, Rosie sat on the edge of the dock, letting her feet dangle over the water.

"You okay?" Carter asked as she sat down next to her.

"I am sad," Rosie admitted. She stared into the murky lake. Ducks floated lazily on the water. Dragonflies hovered in the air. A boat with two fishermen, their lines cast, bobbed in the distance. "I will miss this place. I will miss you, Carter."

"I can't believe I'm saying this, but I'm going to miss you, too," Carter said. She was silent for a moment. "Rosie, I need you to do me a big favor before you go."

"Anything," Rosie promised.

"You said it's a princess's job to help people."

Rosie smiled, remembering all that she and Carter had accomplished. "That's true. It is."

Carter tucked her hair behind her ears. "Well, the dance is tomorrow night, and there are some people I want to help. I want to make this a special night for them, and for all of us. Will you stay until then? Please, just for them."

Rosie hesitated. One more day would not make a big difference. It was the least she could do for Carter.

$\mathcal{B}$ack in Costa Luna, Señor Elegante walked briskly to keep up with General Kane.

"And you're sure about this dance?" the general asked him.

"Absolutely," Señor Elegante assured him. "I feel that in one way I am betraying my queen, but I thought you should know. For the good of Costa Luna."

General Kane gave a satisfied nod. "You did the right thing by coming to me, señor." He turned to Dimitri the guardsman, who was standing nearby. "Fuel the jet. Tell the pilot we will be flying to Louisiana." And then the two men continued down the hallway to Señor Elegante's studio inside the palace.

"A lovely color," General Kane said, fingering the material that was draped over a dress form.

"Caribbean blue, General," Señor Elegante said. "To complement Princess Rosalinda's skin tone."

The general sniffed. He obviously could care less for things of beauty. "Well, back to work. You have a dress to finish." He exited the studio, and Señor Elegante rolled out another dress form. This one had a pale pink dress on it.

"Two, actually," Señor Elegante said with a smile. The princess's friend had come up with a most ingenious plan. It would involve much work and a covert trip to the post office. But if it worked?

Costa Luna would be safe once more.

*M*uch to Carter's relief, everything was going like clockwork. A huge delivery box had arrived—the contents of which were absolutely perfect. She'd spoken to her bus driver, Helen, who was more than happy to help. And all the girls she and Rosie had reached out to at school were also eager to help Carter and Rosie in whatever way they could.

Finally it was the day of the dance.

Back in Costa Luna, Rosie had a hair and makeup person at her disposal. Here in Louisiana things were a little different. Carter had gone to the one person who knew more about beauty than anyone she could think of.

Her bus driver, Helen.

Helen arrived in the school bus and came walking up to the cabin carrying a giant tackle box. But the box was stocked with the most amazing assortment of makeup, hair accessories, and jewelry that Carter had ever seen.

She and Rosie sat at the kitchen table while Helen worked her magic.

"Okay, Carter, how about you?" Helen asked. "Up? Down? French twist?"

Carter smiled. "I want the same as Rosie. If it's all right with you?" she asked her friend.

Rosie touched her just-styled updo. "I would be honored, Carter."

Carter sat back in her seat. No matter what style Rosie had chosen, Carter would have asked Helen for the same thing.

Because for tonight, Carter had to look as much like Rosie as she possibly could.

The next hour was filled with serious primping. Helen styled Carter's hair just like Rosie's. She gave them each a manicure and pedicure with pretty pink polish. She applied their makeup with a light hand.

And then there was just one more thing to

do. "Hmmm," Carter said, pretending to be deep in thought. She was wearing a pair of old jeans and one of her dad's plaid shirts. "Something's missing, but I just can't put my finger on it."

Rosie stared down at her clothes—a pair of Carter's sweatpants and a hoodie. "What are we going to wear?" she asked, dismayed.

Carter went to her room and slid a box out from under the bed. She lifted the lid to reveal two beautiful dresses, one pink, one blue.

Rosie gasped. "Where did you get them?"

Carter gave a little shrug. "You said Mr. Elegante was the one to call in an emergency. "

Rosie was overjoyed. "Carter, you are brilliant!"

Carter took out the pink dress and handed it to Rosie. "This one's yours," she said. "He said pink was a great color on you."

"Thank you, Carter," Rosie said, choking up. "This will be a night that I'll always remember." She hugged her friend tightly.

"Let's hope so," Carter said, hugging Rosie just as hard. She took a deep breath. In a few hours all her preparations would result in a wonderful success . . . or a major failure.

Suddenly, Margaret, along with several other girls from school, appeared in the doorway. They had been waiting on the bus.

"Ummm, are you guys ready for us? It's getting kind of late."

Helen plucked brushes and eye shadows from her kit. "Come on in, girls," she called. "Helen's House of Beauty is open for business."

Carter and Rosie watched as one excited girl after another crowded into the small room. For most of the girls, it was the first time any of them had been given a royal beauty treatment.

Being a princess was pretty cool.

$\mathcal{D}$usk was falling as Carter stood wearing the beautiful blue dress and looking at her reflection in her bedroom mirror. Rosie stood beside her, radiant in pink.

"What do you think, Dad?" Carter asked her father.

"I think we have a problem," he said, his face serious.

Carter looked down at her dress.

"I might have to stop calling you 'pal,'" he said, smiling.

Carter grinned. That was one problem she could handle. When her dad got a work call a few moments later, she assured him they were fine. "You go ahead," she said.

"You sure?" her dad asked.

"Of course! We're not kids," Carter replied.

Her dad nodded. "Have a good time. And be careful." He gave her a big hug. Carter pulled away just as Helen popped into the room.

"All right, Your Highnesses, time's a-wastin'. That dance starts in ten minutes." She gave Carter and Rosie each a beautiful mask.

Carter held it up to her face. Everything was going according to her plan—so far.

Chapter 12

The night should have been perfect. Chelsea was wearing a gorgeous dress, her hair was shimmering, and her lips were perfectly glossed. And then she saw the bus.

A yellow school bus had just pulled into the parking lot, and beautiful girls wearing jaw-dropping dresses and masks were disembarking.

"Masks!" Chelsea shrieked from the passenger seat in Donny's convertible. Her hand flew up instinctively to her bare face. "Nobody said anything about masks!"

Donny couldn't respond. He was too busy gaping. "Wow."

On the side of the parking lot came another "wow" from Ed, who had his video camera ready and rolling.

Furious, Chelsea punched Donny in the arm. How dare her date look at another girl. Make that fifteen girls! Donny got out of the car, pushing past Ed.

"Out of the way, doofus," he said rudely, as he and a group of guys followed the mysterious masked girls into the dance.

You have got to be kidding me, Chelsea thought, shoving the door open. Her dress caught on the handle and she wrenched it free. Then she found herself losing her balance and falling facedown on the grass.

"Are you okay?" Ed asked, rushing over to help her up.

Chelsea pushed him away, spitting a piece of grass from her mouth. She didn't want stupid Ed's help. She wanted revenge on whomever had decided masks were part of the dress code for the homecoming dance . . . and why no one had bothered to tell her.

$\mathcal{T}$he dance was in full swing. The decorations looked beautiful, and everyone was having a great time munching on snacks and working up a sweat on the dance floor. Carter and Rosie were giving two underclassmen a thrill by dancing with them.

"Okay, freshmen, I think I can take it from here," Donny said, full of confidence as he strode up to Carter's dance partner.

Shrugging dejectedly, the guy started to walk away. "No, wait," Carter called to him.

Donny looked stunned. "Carter, what's the problem? I thought we had, you know, something."

Carter shook her head. "Uh, no. Actually, we don't."

But Donny wouldn't let it go. "Okay, what's up?" he asked, his voice accusing. "Isn't this what you've been waiting for, since, like, third grade?"

And just like that, Carter's interest in Donny evaporated for good. "Before I put on this dress, you could never even remember my name," she told him, her eyes narrowing. "I might be a princess tonight, but I'll always be Bait Girl, too. And proud of it."

Donny shook his head. "You're making a huge mistake, Carter."

Carter's lips curled into a smile. "No, Donny. I don't think I am." She watched as he slunk back to his friends, then turned to Rosie.

"You deserve better than him," Rosie said.

Carter nodded. "I know. Too bad it took this long to realize it." Being around Rosie had brought out the best in Carter. And she knew she deserved someone who really cared about her—not some big-headed jerk who treated girls with disrespect. She gave Rosie a nudge. "Now go. Be a princess. Have a good time."

As Rosie flitted off, Carter began searching

the room. She had set a trap in order to lure someone there. With Señor Elegante's help, the bait should work perfectly.

He had to have fallen for the trick. He had to be here.

Rosie's life depended on it.

$\mathcal{B}$rooke was applying another coat of strawberry lip gloss when the bathroom door crashed open. Brooke's eyes widened. It was Chelsea . . . but it didn't look like Chelsea. Her dress was ripped, her hair was a mess, and her makeup was smeared.

"What happened to you?" Brooke asked.

Chelsea just growled. "Shut up and fix me."

Wow, that was kind of mean. Brooke frowned, but she took a comb out of her small purse and started to fix her friend's hair.

"Did you get me a crown?" Brooke asked.

"Who cares?" Chelsea snapped. "In a few minutes it won't matter anyway. I'll be the queen, and this whole thing will be over."

Brooke froze. "I thought we were in this together."

Chelsea looked at her in the mirror. "We are." She held out her hand. "Lip gloss."

The unfairness of her situation swept over Brooke then. "No," she said.

"What?"

Brooke held her ground. "I said no. You can't use my lip gloss anymore."

Chelsea looked aghast. "But I have to look good. I'm a *princess*," she said.

"A terrible one," Brooke blurted out, surprising even herself. "A princess is supposed to be a girl of exemplary character. A role model. But you—you're not kind, honest, or charitable in any way. You're not even *nice*." Her chin began to quiver. "I don't think I want to be your friend anymore."

Chelsea rolled her eyes. "Aw, Brookie."

Brooke turned away. "Don't call me that." She walked out, her crownless head held high.

* * *

Carter and Rosie were standing off to the side of the dance floor watching the crowd when Margaret approached them. "Carter, Rosie, I just want to thank you for tonight. I never thought I could look beautiful, or feel like it, for that matter."

Carter smiled. "You are beautiful, Margaret."

"*Eres muy bonita,*" Rosie added.

Margaret fluffed her hair. "And thanks for not calling me Muffy."

Carter shrugged. "Uh . . . no problem." As Margaret blended back into the crowd, Carter could feel her pulse begin to quicken. She wanted so badly to tell Rosie what was about to happen.

But she couldn't.

Outside the gym, Chelsea walked briskly down the hall. She spotted several security guards walking toward the entrance. She hurried ahead and stepped in front of them. "There you are, finally!"

127

"You do not understand," one of them said. He frowned. "I am—"

Chelsea cut him off. "Security. I know. You're late." She took in their overly formal garb. "And what is with these uniforms? Nobody's wearing berets this year." She blew out her breath, exasperated. "Just stay out here and make sure no one gets in if they're not a Lake Monroe student. Got it?"

The guard who had spoken before nodded. "Yes. That will be fine. Enjoy your dance."

And with that, Chelsea flitted inside the gym to greet her royal subjects.

*O*h. My. Gosh. They're here! It worked! Carter thought. She was thrilled.

There in the gym doorway were several men that Carter knew were General Kane and his soldiers. This was no joke. This was the moment she'd been dreading and waiting for all at once. She stopped staring and ducked back into the dance, crossing the floor to the group of fifteen masked princesses.

"He's going to announce the winner," Carter said, pointing to Principal Burkle at the podium. "Masks on, everyone."

And it was just in time, for at that very moment General Kane entered the gym with his soldiers.

"May I have your attention, please? Quiet, please!"

The DJ stopped his music. The lights dimmed, and a spotlight fell on Principal Burkle. People gathered together in small groups, lowering their voices.

Carter stood off to the side. Her Caribbean blue dress glimmered in the dim light. Suddenly, she felt two sets of rough hands grab her. The soldiers had fallen for her ruse. They thought she was Rosie! Without saying a word, they began ushering her to the door.

Stay calm, stay calm, she thought. The words were a mantra in her nervous brain. She had to keep cool. She could hear the principal making the announcement as they walked briskly down the school corridor.

"The winner is . . . Princess Rosie González!"

A corner of Carter's heart filled with happiness . . . the rest was packed with fear.

"Your mother will be so pleased to see you, *Princesa*," General Kane said scornfully. "She has been so sad."

Carter said nothing. She kept her eyes on the ground, trying not to trip. They were walking so fast. As they passed the pool, one of the soldiers gave her arm a hard yank.

"Hurry!" General Kane barked. "Before anyone notices she is missing."

No one had . . . yet.

Back in the gym, cheers were erupting from the students over their choice for homecoming queen.

"Rosie?" called out Principal Burkle, shading his eyes and peering into the audience. "Are you out there?"

The spotlight found her, and she made her

way to the front of the stage. "Where's Carter?" she asked Margaret, who was standing at the front. "I want her to be here with me." But Margaret didn't know. Rosie walked onto the stage, still trying to find her friend in the crowd of students.

When the principal placed the crown on her head, Rosie realized she had to get back into the moment. "Thank you," she said to everyone. "Thank you very much. I am extremely honored to be your queen." As they all applauded, Rosie kept searching for Carter. "Lake Monroe is very different from my home . . . in Iowa," Rosie continued. "Since I've been here I've learned many wonderful things. Most importantly, I've learned about friendship and about loyalty and trust, and that those are not things we are given but things we must earn."

Rosie took a deep breath. She was filled with affection for her new friends and this place that had so warmly embraced her. "So I want to thank Carter Mason for teaching me this, and for being my friend. Carter, where are you?" She scanned the room yet again. Where could she be?

"That was so beautiful, Rosie," Margaret told her as she exited the stage.

"Thank you," Rosie said, but her mind was focused on finding her friend. She was beginning to get a bad feeling about Carter's absence.

All of a sudden, the two freshmen she and Carter had danced with earlier came running up to her. "These two crazy-looking security guards just took Carter out of here," one of them said breathlessly.

"She must have really done something gnarly," the other one added, his eyes round as saucers.

In a flash, Rosie realized what was going on. General Kane and his men had found her. Or so they thought.

Rosie ran for the door and raced down the hallway. When she got outside, she raced across the pool deck.

And then, unexpectedly, Chelsea popped up in front of her. "Hold it right there, Princess."

"What is it, Chelsea?" Rosie asked. There was no time for petty arguing.

"My crown. Hand it over," Chelsea ordered.

"Chelsea, please—" Rosie began, trying to get past her.

The girl would not move. "You're not going anywhere until you give me that."

Rosie whipped the crown off her head and pretended she was going to throw it in the pool. As she predicted, Chelsea lunged for it—then slipped and fell into the water.

"Sorry!" Rosie said, stifling a laugh.

Chelsea's arms windmilled in the water as her poofy dress floated up to the surface. "You are soooo going to pay for that."

But Rosie was already running away.

She found General Kane, his men, and Carter out on the school courtyard. A helicopter was waiting for them.

"General Kane!" she shouted.

He stopped and turned to see her standing there alone, without her mask.

He smiled coldly. "Well, it appears as if everyone wants to be a princess. Unfortunately it is time for the masquerade to end."

Carter took off her mask. "What are you doing?" she cried to Rosie. "The plan was working perfectly."

Rosie ran to her. "It was a brave plan, Carter. But this is my fight, not yours."

The helicopter started up. "You don't have to go with them," Carter pleaded, grabbing her arm.

"Enough!" General Kane shouted. "As the *princesa* so eloquently pointed out, this is not your fight."

Rosie bit her lip as General Kane pulled her toward the helicopter. She had tried so hard to protect her family and her country, but it was not to be. As the chopper's doors slid open, Rosie gasped. Inside were not more of Kane's soldiers—but the Director of the International Princess Protection Program, two operatives, and Mr. Mason!

"General Kane," Mr. Mason said, "good to see you again."

General Kane looked furious. "What is the meaning of this? You are interfering with official business of the sovereign land of Costa Luna."

From the shadows, more operatives materialized. They grabbed General Kane's guards.

"Maybe this will fly in your country," Mr. Mason said. "But here, we call it kidnapping. We're turning you over to the authorities."

Without warning, General Kane made a break for it, tearing across the school courtyard. And on his heels was Mr. Mason. In seconds, he had tackled the general to the ground.

Rosie and Carter exchanged happy glances.

"How does it feel to be brought to justice by a sixteen-year-old girl, General?" Mr. Mason asked, slapping a pair of handcuffs on General Kane's wrists.

"Not so hot," he muttered.

And finally, after weeks in exile, Rosie was able to take a deep, calming breath. It was over.

Chapter

13

$\mathcal{C}$arter's plan hadn't gone quite as she had imagined it. But the end result was all she could have dreamed of.

"I cannot believe you did this all for me," Rosie whispered, hugging her tightly as they stood in the moonlight.

Carter hugged her back. "That's what princesses do, right? They do for others."

"Yes, they do," Rosie agreed. "And you are truly a princess, Carter Mason."

Rosie reached up, removed her crown, and

placed it on Carter's head. "This rightfully belongs to you."

"Hold it! Nobody goes anywhere! Nobody moves!" It wasn't a soldier or a secret agent. It was something far scarier—Chelsea.

She came to a stop, panting and soaking wet. She reached over and grabbed the crown from Carter. "I'll take that," she screeched, on the verge of tears. And then she limped away on her broken heels.

As Rosie made a move to go after her, Carter held her back. "Let her go," she said generously. "She needs it way more than I do."

Mr. Mason was motioning for Carter to join him. His expression was grim.

"I am in so much trouble," she whispered to Rosie before walking slowly across the pavement to her father.

"Carter, what were you thinking?" he shouted, running his hands through his hair.

Carter swallowed. "I was thinking I'd be the perfect bait? Get it? I'm the bait girl."

He drew his lips together. "I get it. Why didn't you just come to me?"

Carter shrugged. "You would never have let me do it."

Her father sighed. "You're lucky I was here, Carter."

Carter knew he was right. She grinned. "I knew you would be. You're always there for me. You rescue princesses, and tonight, *I'm* a princess."

Her dad couldn't stay angry with her for long, especially when things had worked out as wonderfully as they had. He smiled. "You and me, pal."

Carter melted into his strong arms. "You and me, Dad."

*R*osie returned home to Costa Luna, and soon order was restored. The people were happy to have their beloved *princesa* home.

And then, at last, the day had arrived. Rosalinda's coronation.

Carter practically had to pinch herself to believe it. Here she was, at the Costa Luna Royal Palace!

And even more amazing—she was on the dais next to Rosie. She held her breath as Rosie, looking gorgeous, bowed her head to receive the royal crown. Rosie's mother sat alongside her, wearing a beautiful gown and beaming with pride. And behind her stood her personal guard—Mr. Mason.

The archbishop faced the crowd. "I present to you Queen Rosalinda Marie Montoya Fiore of Costa Luna!"

Rosie turned to smile at Carter, and Carter grinned back, reaching up to touch the locket she now wore—an identical match to her friend's.

My friend, the queen! she thought.

A string quartet began to play, and the crowd erupted in polite applause. Suddenly, a shout rang out. "Long live Queen Rosie!" It was Ed— one of the few special guests attending from

Lake Monroe High School along with Carter.

Everyone turned to stare at him—until Carter stood up on the dais. "Long live Queen Rosie!" she declared, meeting Ed's look with a smile.

And then to Carter's delight, cheers went up from the crowd. *"Que viva la Reina Rosalinda!"*

Rosie walked over, and she and Carter did their fist bump.

Friends to the end.

But it was just the beginning.